For my children
I'll always be here to listen
- KB

Our Feelings

Written & illustrated by Katie Budge

When I feel...

I feel like...

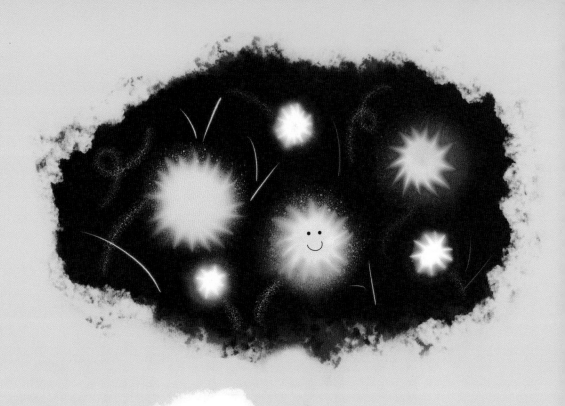

When I feel happy, I feel like a firework,
like a bright and colourful spark.
I burst and fizz, zip and whizz
and I glow through the dark.

When I feel happy, I feel like a rainbow
my beautiful colours shine high.
With red and blue and purple too
I brighten up the sky.

When I feel sad, I feel like a cloud
a dark, heavy cloud full of rain.
I float on by, in a darkened sky,
and pour down again and again.

When I feel sad, I feel like a teddy bear
that's been left behind at home.
Up on a shelf, all by myself,
I feel so glum and alone.

When I feel excited, I feel like a monkey
swinging up high in the trees.
I swing high and low and around I go
and upside down if I please.

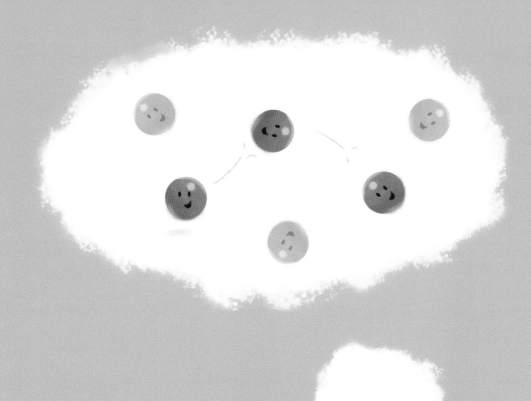

When I feel excited, I feel like a bouncy ball
I bounce and boing and bound.
I spring in the air, without any care,
I just can't keep myself on the ground.

When I feel angry, I feel like a wasp
I buzz round on a stormy day.
I beat my wing and I want to sting,
EVERYTHING that gets in my way!

When I feel angry, I feel like a bubbling pot,
with thick clouds of steam in the air.
Bubbles pop as I blow my top
and hot water spills everywhere!

When I feel scared, I feel like a mouse
being chased by a VERY big cat.
Hidden away is where I stay,
hoping I don't get trapped.

When I feel worried, I feel like jelly on a plate,
I feel so wobbly inside.
I shake and shiver, quake and quiver,
I just want to run and hide.

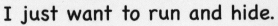

When I feel proud I feel like a giant,
I stand tall for everyone to see.
I smile and wave, feeling brave
with everyone cheering for me.

When I feel proud I feel like a lion,
not one for being shy.
My smile is wide, beaming with pride
standing tall with my head held high.

When I feel anxious, I feel like a knotted ball
tied up together too tight.
I try to untangle, I pull from each angle
but I can't seem to make myself right.

When I feel anxious, I feel like a washing machine,
I spin round and round and round.
It makes me feel sick, it makes me breathe quick,
I just want to shut off and wind down.

When I feel loved, I feel like a flower
I stand beautifully on display.
Kissed by the sun, the rain is so fun,
I grow more and more every day.

When I feel loved, I feel like a puppy,
with everyone caring for me.
I get lots of cuddles and tight, warm snuggles
There's no where else I'd rather be!

We all have feelings for us to share
with family, friends and teachers too.
So any feelings, we don't understand,
they can **help** us to know what to do.

Feelings are perfectly normal
each one of us have them inside.
They change, just like the weather,
but feelings are **never** to hide.

Share them always, whatever they are
with someone you know and trust.
No matter what you are feeling,
sharing them is **always** a must.

All books by Katie Budge can be found on
www.amazon.co.uk

Katie Budge Books

Facebook: KTBudgeBooks
Instagram: @kt_budge_books

Printed in Great Britain
by Amazon